11/49

PA

SWEET PEA'S CHRISTMAS

Marcia Leiter

Sweet Pea Tales
Book 2

SWEET PEA'S CHRISTMAS
Story, Illustrations and Book Design
by Marcia Leiter

Birdberry Press Copyright 2016

Also by Marcia Leiter:
Sweet Pea's Tale of Too Many Tomatoes!
Sweet Pea's Journey

Visit Sweet Pea at
sweet-pea.net

Dedicated to
Barbara

Who fills each Christmas
with joy
and good things to eat

Once there was a little bunny named
Sweet Pea who lived in a quiet
cozy hole by the stream.

The day after
Thanksgiving she reached into her
mailbox and pulled out a BIG fat envelope.

On page **7** of her Aunt Lennie's holiday newsletter was a

SURPRISE.

A few days later she looked at the calendar. It was DECEMBER the 1st.

"Soon it will be Christmas!" she said. "I must get ready!"

The next day she went up to her musty dusty attic...

...found the big brown Christmas barrel.

...and bumped it down the stairs.

Everything was broken, tangled or mildewed.

On December 3
Sweet Pea received
another surprise.
"GOODNESS!"
she said, and
immediately
began housecleaning.

She scrubbed

and

mopped

and polished

all day long.

On the 4th Sweet Pea cut the lowest branches from her holly tree to make a wreath for her front door.

On the 5th she made 139 golden drippy candles to light her windows.

On December 6
Sweet Pea did not do any holiday preparations.
She went to a birthday party instead.

The next day she worked extra hard from dawn to dusk chopping wood for her fireplace.

On December 8 she tried to make Christmas cards.
Instead she made a big mess.

"NOBUNNY is getting a card from me
THIS year!" she said.

On December **9** Sweet Pea untangled 123 Twinklefly Lights and strung them all around. They were beautiful.

On the 10th she vacuumed the attic...

On the 11th she washed six dozen sheets with matching pillow cases...

...and set up a very long row of cots borrowed from String Bean's cranky Uncle Castor.

...and hung them up to dry.

December 12 was rainy. Sweet Pea sat by the fire and made 82 little stockings. No two were alike.

On the **13th** she found her roof had leaked all over the freshly made beds.

While she fixed it String Bean washed everything all over again.

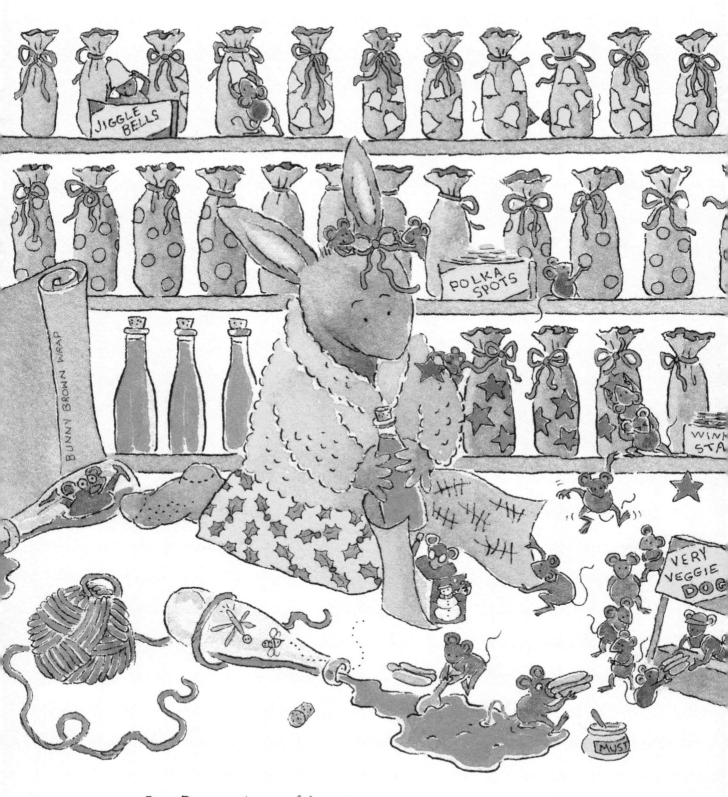

On December 14 she wrapped 96 bottles of homemade ketchup in brown paper tied with red yarn.

On the **15**th Sweet Pea knitted 46 little scarves,
46 tiny caps and 46 pairs of itty bitty mittens.

On December 16 Sweet Pea counted
ONE HUNDRED AND THIRTY SEVEN
guests coming for Christmas and only
NINE days left!

On the 17th she pulled on her messy Mud Muggers, slogged through the muddy woods and cut one small branch off a very TALL PINE for her Christmas tree...

Oh Christmas Tree Oh

HARES' SAWS

...and then took a nap.

On the **18**th of December Sweet Pea baked cookies all day long.

Gingerbread Bunnies

Carrot Yums

and Cinnamon Mice.

On December 19 she went to the Christmas Mart
to fetch goodies for 156 little stockings.

On the 20th Sweet Pea decorated her tree.

She sliced oranges into stained glass windows,

cut snowflakes from old envelopes,

strung cranberry garlands,

FIRE CHIEF

thwt

and made tiny candles to light the tree.

On December the 21st while reading the morning paper...

...she thought of something IMPORTANT.

String Bean promptly put up 9 more potting sheds.

FORM A SINGLE LINE

Three days before Christmas Sweet Pea began to fill up her pantry. She baked

4 kinds of bread

SOURDOUGH

RYE

STOLLEN

WHOLE WHEAT

WILDBERRY

CHERRY

SWEET POTATO

3 kinds of pie

DEC 22

2 kinds of cake

LEMON SPONGE

CARROT

and 1 genuine Christmas Pudding.

On December **23** she got up very early and started chopping vegetables for the soup.

She chopped all day and into the night.

On Christmas Eve Sweet Pea
woke up late.

"TOO MUCH TO DO!"
"NO TIME! NO TIME!"
she said as she
scampered about

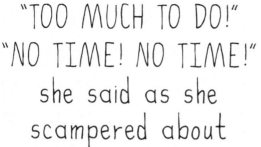

setting tables,

pumping water,

stuffing stockings,

and hauling wood.

At midnight she took a bath

and flopped into bed.

During
the
night
a
snowflake
fell...
...then
another
and
another.

When Sweet Pea woke up on
Christmas Morning
her whole hole was dark.
A cold wind was whooshing down the chimney.

"No one will be able to come," said Sweet Pea.
She sat by the cold fireplace
all morning and stared at

182 lumpy
stockings,

MERRY ?C

182 empty bowls, and
182 tiny candles ready to light on the tree.

Then, suddenly there was a big THUD as String Bean landed on a pile of soot.

"Sorry," he said.
"I couldn't find your door."
"How did you get here?" she said.

"SNOWSHOES!" said String Bean.

"You better get out
of those pajamas
and get busy!"

While String Bean
shoveled
a tunnel
from the
front door...

...Sweet Pea flew around the house.

THEN she opened the door.

STOP STOP

GLUG
GLUG

Soon her tidy hole was full to bursting with
TOO MANY BUNNIES...

...and too much MESS!

But Sweet Pea didn't mind a bit.

About the
Author
Illustrator

Marcia Leiter
loves Christmas time.
She has done (almost) all
the things that Sweet Pea did in the
story... except Sweet Pea had more guests.
Marcia used to make story books for her
children and friends. You can make a story
too, for someone you love. All you need
is paper, pencils, crayons and some quiet
time. Now close your eyes and just start
drawing. Let your imagination fly...

A CHRISTMAS SEEK and FIND

 A red "potting shed"

A little yellow mail box

A purple pilgrim

Too Many Tomatoes!

A broken blue ornament

Baby bunny... ...mouse

 A poke in the bottom

A candy cane candle

Far away Bean house

Log house tea time

 A bee stuck in glue

A bath in green paint

A candle in the window

An eight-legged critter

Twinkleflies  in love

 Trouble with s'mores

Sheet drying in the sun

A very sticky bell-hat

 Wisebunny bearing a gift

Rudy the Red-Nosed Bunny

A row of BLUE teeth!

A happy cookie

A puzzle or two

A handsome fire hat

The morning news

Lemon slice and cherries

 Hot chile peppers!

A lettuce dress

A smart fishie

A bee in a bubble bath

 A tiny rocking cradle

A green skier

A bee with mittens

 A twinklefly reflection

A fallen  yellow halo

A surprised ornament

 Teatime for bees

Bunnies in a skiboat

WAKE UP they're HERE

 A sleepy mouse in a hat

 A marathon mouse

A big green bow

A blue scarf-blanket

A red-eyed bunny doll

 Shake the ketchup bottle

Christmas  carolers

A silver jingle bell

 A striped stuffed stocking

A big bowl of lettuce

A bunch of mistletoe

 Toasting meecemallows

A one-legged bunny?

 Beezzzzzzz

Shepherds

How to make Sweet Pea's Ornaments

Stained Glass Windows

Get some oranges, lemons or limes.
Have a GROWNUP slice them thin.
Poke ornament hooks through them.
Hang on a string in your window to dry.

 ### Snowflakes

Get some paper... white or colors.
Trace around a bowl. Cut out the circle.
Fold it in half, then thirds like a pie.
Cut out pieces with safety scissors.
                    Open it up!

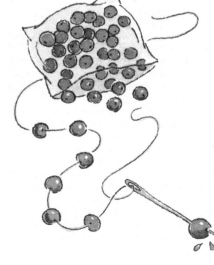

Cranberry Garland

Get a bag of cranberries.
Get a dull, fat needle and thread it.
        Poke through each berry to string.

Sweet Pea's Gingerbread Bunnies

STIR TOGETHER
until creamy ▶

½ cup butter, softened
½ cup sugar
¼ cup real molasses
¼ cup agave nectar
    (or corn syrup)
½ egg
1 Tablespoon vinegar

STIR TOGETHER
until mixed well ▶

2 ½ cups flour
¼ teaspoon baking soda
¼ teaspoon salt
½ teaspoon ginger
½ teaspoon cinnamon
½ teaspoon cloves

Stir dry ingredients into wet. Mix well. Chill 3 or more hours.
Work with ¼ of dough at a time, keeping the rest chilled.
Use lots of flour on a wooden board and roll out ¼" thick.
Cut with floured cutter, place on lightly greased sheets.
Bake at 375 in center of oven ... 5 minutes for large cookies,
3 minutes for tiny ones. Cool and decorate with icing. YUM.

CPSIA information can be obtained
at www.ICGtesting.com
Printed in the USA
LVHW052259161019
634422LV00002B/2/P